Atlanta Hawks

Richard Rambeck

CREATIVE EDUCATION

Published by Creative Education
123 South Broad Street, Mankato, Minnesota 56001
Creative Education is an imprint of The Creative Company

Designed by Rita Marshall

Photos by: Allsport Photography, Associated Press/Wide World Photos,
Focus on Sports, NBA Photos, UPI/Corbis Bettmann, and SportsChrome.

Photo page 1: Alan Henderson
Photo title page: Steve Smith

Library of Congress Cataloging-in-Publication Data

Rambeck, Richard.
Atlanta Hawks / Richard Rambeck.
p. cm. — (NBA today)
Summary: Describes the background and history of the Atlanta Hawks
pro basketball team to 1997.
ISBN 0-88682-865-1

1. Atlanta Hawks (Basketball team)—History—Juvenile literature.
[1. Atlanta Hawks (Basketball team)—History. 2. Basketball—History.]
I. Title. II. Series: NBA today (Mankato, Minn.)

GV885.52.A7R36 1997   96-53185
796.323'64'09758231—dc21

First edition

5 4 3 2

The city of Atlanta has a proud history, and one of its brightest moments dates back to the Civil War. On the night of November 14, 1864, General William Sherman and his Union troops marched on Atlanta and set the city on fire. Throughout the night, orange flames lit up the Georgia sky. By morning, Atlanta was almost burned to the ground. The residents of Atlanta immediately began rebuilding their city from the ashes. Their heroic effort came to symbolize the determination and pride of the South.

Atlanta is now one of the largest metropolitan areas in the country. It is the capital of Georgia, and the cultural and fi-

All-time great Cliff Hagan.

nancial capital of the southeastern United States. Atlanta is also known for its rich sports tradition. In 1996, Atlanta hosted the Summer Olympics, making it an internationally recognized sports center. The city is home to professional football, baseball, and basketball franchises, all of which were established in the late 1960s.

Atlanta's pro basketball team, the Hawks, has a history as rich as the city's. The franchise began in 1949 as an original member of the National Basketball Association (NBA). For nearly 20 years, it moved from place to place in the Midwest, finally settling in the south in 1968. The Atlanta Hawks have never won an NBA championship, but for nearly three decades the club has showcased such talented players as Lou Hudson, "Pistol" Pete Maravich, Bob Pettit, Cliff Hagan, Dominique Wilkins, Moses Malone, Spud Webb, Kevin Willis, and Stacey Augmon. Now the Hawks have the NBA's winningest coach, Lenny Wilkens, and one of the NBA's best centers in Dikembe Mutombo. Together they hope to bring an NBA title home to the Omni in Atlanta.

MEANDERING THROUGH THE MIDWEST

The franchise that became the Atlanta Hawks was originally called the Tri-Cities Blackhawks. Its home was in the three neighboring cities of Moline, Illinois; Rock Island, Illinois; and Davenport, Iowa. After two seasons, the team moved to Milwaukee and dropped the "Black" from its name.

The Milwaukee Hawks had a new 10,000 seat arena. Unfortunately, the Milwaukee fans didn't get a winning team. The Hawks were among the worst teams in the NBA, losing

Offensive standout Lou Hudson.

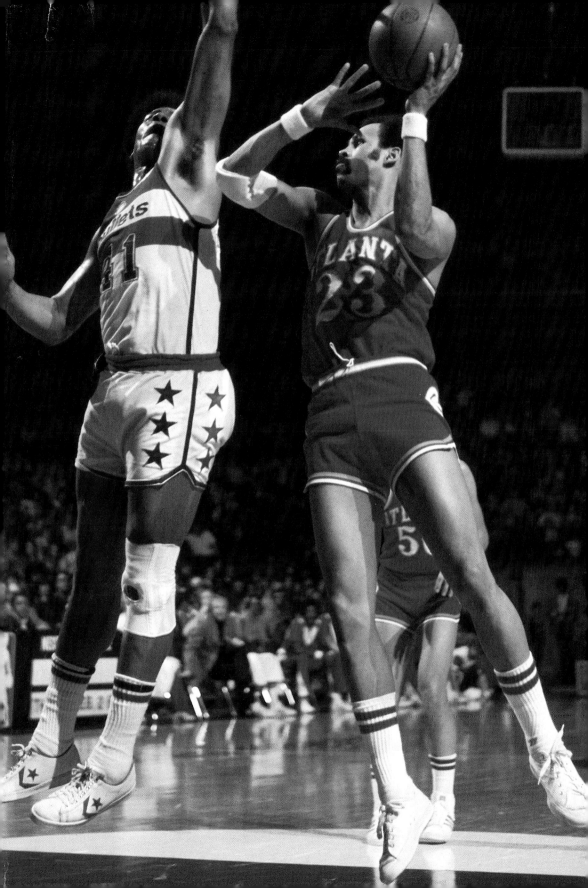

190 games in four seasons. After a while, the fans stopped coming to watch the hapless Hawks.

During the 1954–55 season, owner Ben Kerner realized his club would fold unless he did something quickly. Kerner had an idea. He noted that the major league baseball team known as the St. Louis Browns had just moved to Baltimore to become the Orioles. "If we move the Hawks to St. Louis," Kerner said, "maybe we can convert some of those fans to basketball."

1 9 5 6

MVP Bob Pettit led the NBA in scoring and rebounding.

Kerner's Hawks did indeed begin the 1955–56 NBA season in St. Louis, and the move apparently changed the team's luck. The St. Louis Hawks made the playoffs and defeated the Minneapolis Lakers in the first round. Although they lost in the league semifinals to the Fort Wayne Pistons, the Hawks had established themselves as a team to beat.

PETTIT TAKES THE HAWKS TO THE TOP

One of the main reasons for the success of the St. Louis Hawks was a skinny forward named Bob Pettit. At 6-foot-9 and only 200 pounds, Bob Pettit was considered by many experts to be too thin to be a great NBA player. But Pettit was used to proving himself to others. When he was only 15, Pettit was cut from his high school basketball team. He didn't give up, however. He went home and practiced shooting in his parents' driveway in Baton Rouge, Louisiana. He took thousands of shots at the hoop on the family garage, perfecting an uncanny array of jump shots, hook shots, and inside moves.

Pettit's hard work paid off. He became an outstanding

high school player and then went on to star at Louisiana State University. In his senior year at LSU, Pettit was college basketball's top scorer, averaging 30 points a game. In the 1954 college draft, the Milwaukee Hawks ignored the scouts who said Pettit was too thin. They took the LSU All-American with their first pick. How well did Pettit do? He was named NBA Rookie of the Year in 1954–55 and then, in only his second season, he earned the NBA's Most Valuable Player (MVP) award.

Clyde Lovellette was the first player to win an NBA championship, Olympic gold medal, and NCAA title.

"Everyone said Pettit was too skinny to make it in the NBA," said Hawks coach Red Holzman. "Then the guy averages 25 points and 16 rebounds a game and gets the MVP award. What's everyone going to say now? That the rest of the guys in the league are too fat?"

Pettit explained the secret behind his success. "You go along in life and work hard," he said. "You reach new levels of accomplishment. And with each level you reach, the demands upon you become greater. Your pride increases to meet the demands. You drive yourself harder than before."

Pettit didn't think about failure. "You can't afford negative thinking, so you always believe you will win," Pettit observed. "You build an image of yourself that has nothing to do with ego, but it has to be satisfied. When I fall below what I know I can do, my belly growls and growls. Anytime I'm not playing up to my very best, I can count on a jolt of indigestion."

Pettit consistently played his best, so it was usually the Hawks' opponents who wound up with indigestion. Led by Pettit and forwards Cliff Hagan and Clyde Lovellette, St. Louis won five straight Western Division titles from 1957

The legendary Bob Pettit, a Hawks star of the 1960s.

Glenn "Doc" Rivers, a Hawks sensation in the 1980s.   11

Lenny Wilkens was named an NBA All-Star for the third year in a row.

through 1961. The Hawks advanced to the league championship series four times, and each time they came up against the powerful Boston Celtics. St. Louis lost to Boston three times, but won the NBA title in 1957–58.

During the early 1960s, the Hawks declined slightly—from great to pretty good. Pettit and Hagan were still around to lead the club, and they were joined by such young players as center Zelmo Beaty and guard Lenny Wilkens. Even when Pettit retired in 1965 and Hagan called it quits the following year, the Hawks remained one of the top teams in the Western Division.

In 1967–68, the Hawks seemed to be headed toward a championship. Led by Beaty, Wilkens, and power forward Bill Bridges, they won 11 of their first 12 games. By season's end, St. Louis had posted a 56–26 record, and had earned its first division title in seven years.

It had been 10 years since St. Louis had last won an NBA title, and the team's players and fans were hungry for another. Their hopes were crushed quickly, however, when the San Francisco Warriors upset the Hawks in the first round of the playoffs.

"It was humiliating," said a disappointed Bill Bridges. "The whole season and our great record meant nothing."

It soon would mean even less to the St. Louis fans. Following the 1967–68 season, Hawks owner Ben Kerner decided to sell the team to a group of investors in Atlanta. Kerner explained that a move was necessary because the 9,000-seat arena in St. Louis was too small to enable an NBA club to pay the high salaries of its players. Atlanta basketball

12

fans felt lucky. They were getting a solid NBA team with a successful track record.

The Hawks continued their solid play after the move south. In only their second year in Atlanta, 1969–70, they captured the Western Division title. The club's stars were point guard Walt Hazzard, acrobatic forward Joe Caldwell, and high-scoring guard/forward Lou Hudson—a deadly accurate outside shooter. Unfortunately, these standout players couldn't keep the Hawks from coming apart in the playoffs. After getting past the Chicago Bulls in the first round, Atlanta lost to the Los Angeles Lakers in the division finals.

Lou Hudson, the Hawks' leading scorer, was named to the NBA's All-Rookie team.

MARAVICH BECOMES ATLANTA'S TOP GUN

The loss to the Lakers showed that the Hawks weren't quite championship material. So after the 1969–70 season, Atlanta added a player many experts believed could make the team into a title contender. In the first round of the 1970 college draft, the Hawks selected a sharpshooter known as "Pistol Pete." To this day, nobody has scored more points in college (3,667) than Pete Maravich did for Louisiana State University. The Pistol averaged a remarkable 44.2 points per game over three seasons, and was named College Player of the Year after the 1969–70 season.

Maravich's admirers knew he could do more than just score. "Pete is regarded chiefly as a scorer, a popgun," explained former LSU star Joe Dean. "But his real appeal, the thing that sets him apart, is not his shooting but his passing." Legendary University of Kentucky coach Adolph Rupp also

13

Bill Bridges's 1,233 rebounds set a Hawks record that stood for more than 20 years.

noted that Maravich was "as near a complete ballplayer as you'll ever see anywhere."

Maravich's wide range of skills amazed the experts. "He has the greatest basketball imagination I've ever seen," claimed Bob Ferry, assistant coach and scout for the Baltimore Bullets. "I don't know how he does half the things he does with the ball. He has great quick hands, quick eyes. He's an unbelievable passer and a great middleman on the fast break. He can penetrate with the ball. He can hit the open man. Offensively, I don't think there's a thing he can't do."

Pete Maravich was born to play basketball. His father, Press, who would later coach him at LSU, gave him a ball to play with when he was a toddler. Pete almost never put the ball down. "I guess I love the game of basketball more than anything else in the world," he explained. "From the beginning, it was like an addiction to me, because I played it so much—four to five hours a day. I never really was interested in other sports, or anything else either."

Pete put on a show in Atlanta that lasted four seasons. He combined with Lou Hudson to give the Hawks one of the best backcourts in the NBA.

But Maravich also had his critics. They said he shot too much and that his passes were too flashy. "He scores 50 points," said Boston Celtics guard K.C. Jones, "but he throws up 100 shots." Maravich admitted that he had a tendency to showboat, but that was what set him apart from other players. "I guess there are several tons of ham in me," he said. "That must be obvious. I recognized early that basketball, more than any other team game, gives a guy the opportunity to be a showman. You can do more stuff, more antics. Any

The fabulous Pistol Pete.

Dan Roundfield led the Hawks in blocked shots with 176.

one guy has much more of a chance to put on a show. That really is what basketball is for me—an entertainment, a chance to express myself."

Maravich learned to look for his teammates, particularly Hudson. "I just try to get open," explained Hudson. "That's the only way a guy like Pete will notice you and throw you the ball." Hudson and Maravich both averaged more than 25 points a game during the 1972–73 season, as the Hawks finished second in their division.

The two Atlanta guards had another banner year in 1973–74, but the Hawks disappointed their fans with another second-place finish in their division. The Hawks weren't a bad club, but the team wasn't a championship contender either.

In an effort to build a winner, Pete Maravich was traded to the New Orleans Jazz for players and draft picks. The trade had an immediate effect on both teams. The young Jazz gained an electric star who helped them draw fans. The Hawks, meanwhile, started to slip in the standings.

Atlanta spent most of the late 1970s trying to build another championship-caliber team. After years of disappointing results, the Hawks—behind the solid play of forwards John Drew and Dan Roundfield, and guard Eddie Johnson—finally won the NBA Central Division title in 1979–80. Atlanta eventually lost to the powerful Philadelphia 76ers in the playoffs, but their hopes were high for the future. What did the future bring? The Hawks finished second in the division in both 1981–82 and 1982–83, but the team had little success in the playoffs, losing in the first round both times.

Though the Hawks ended the 1982–83 season in disappointing fashion, they found a new star in rookie sensation Jacques Dominique Wilkins. Wilkins had come out of the University of Georgia with a reputation as a great scorer and an even better leaper. Nicknamed the "Human Highlight Film," Wilkins was known for his spectacular slam dunks, each one worthy of being broadcast on sports highlight shows. During his rookie season, Wilkins averaged more than 17 points and nearly six rebounds per game. In his second and third years, his offensive statistics continued to improve. He averaged 21.6 and 27.4 points per game, respectively, during those two campaigns.

Wayne "Tree" Rollins's blocked-shot percentage of 4.29 was the best in the NBA.

Wilkins was doing great individually, but the Hawks weren't winning. That fact disappointed the young star. He wanted to let fans know that he was more than a showman. He wanted to prove that he was one of the best players in the NBA, and that he could help his team become a winner, too. Wilkins achieved both of these goals during the 1985–86 season. He won the NBA scoring title with a 30.3 average and led the Hawks to a second-place finish in their division with a 50–32 record—a 16-game improvement over the previous season.

"I always thought he could win the scoring title," recalled Hawks president Stan Kasten. "But I wondered if he could do it with a winning team. Dominique did just that. . . . 'Nique works so hard. He loves the game, and he never takes a night off."

Wilkins took great pride in his accomplishments during

The Hawks establish position (pages 18–19).

the 1985–86 campaign. "This season I wanted to prove I was a total player," he explained. "I wanted to change people's opinion of me. It bothered me that I had never made the All-Star team, that people thought all I could do was dunk. Well, I've proved it now. No question about it."

The 1985–86 season also marked Wilkins's emergence as the Hawks' leader. During his first few years in the pros, Wilkins had been fairly quiet on the court. That changed during the 1985–86 season. "Dominique accepted the responsibility of being our leader, the man who has to get us going," explained Atlanta forward Cliff Levingston.

1 9 8 5

Eddie Johnson recorded 566 assists, leading the Hawks for the third season in a row.

Dominique Wilkins emerged as the team's leader.

One of the players who benefited most from Wilkins's leadership was rookie point guard Spud Webb. "He's been my big brother from day one," Webb recalled. "I don't know how I would have made it without him." They made an odd pair: Wilkins was 6-foot-8, whereas Webb was only 5-foot-7.

Webb was the shortest player in the league, but because of his great speed and jumping ability, he was also one of the most exciting. In his rookie season, Webb amazed almost everyone by winning the NBA's slam-dunk contest during the 1986 All-Star Weekend. Webb had a vertical leap of 42 inches. Despite his size, he could jump more than a foot above the rim. Webb had first dunked during the summer before his senior year in high school. "I must have tried dunking about a thousand times and failed," Spud recalled. "I finally got one. The reaction from the other guys was, 'Well, it's about time.'"

Once Webb proved he could dunk, he then had to prove he could do everything else on the basketball court. After high school, Webb went to Midland College in Texas for two years, where he became a solid point guard. "Spud can direct the team, make assists, and pass on the break as well as anybody I've seen," said Midland coach Jerry Stone. "The jumping ability is just icing on the cake."

Webb then enrolled at North Carolina State. He played well enough there to be selected by the Detroit Pistons in the fourth round of the 1985 NBA draft. But the Pistons told Webb he was unlikely to make the team. They released him,

1 9 8 7

Glenn "Doc" Rivers grabbed 163 steals, leading the team for the second straight year.

21

Spud Webb was a dazzling playmaker.

and Atlanta signed the tiny leaper. For most of his rookie year, Webb sat on the Hawks' bench. Then Doc Rivers, the starting point guard, got hurt. Webb moved into the starting lineup, but he worried that the Hawks would let him go when Rivers came back.

Wilkins told his friend to stop worrying, that he had a place in Atlanta's future. "You think they'd spend all this time on you if they were going to let you go?" Wilkins said. "Besides, you're a player. We've got to keep you." Webb worked hard to show critics that he was more than a sideshow mighty mite who had won the slam-dunk contest. "People talk about my dunking and not the other stuff," Webb complained. "I can pass, jump shoot, dribble, and lead the team. Maybe they [the fans] want entertainment, but I want to be known as a good point guard."

A 30.7 scoring average made Dominique Wilkins second in the NBA.

Webb made his point. After Rivers returned, Webb wasn't cut from the club. Instead, he was moved to the bench and became the team's "super sub." Atlanta coach Mike Fratello put Webb in when he wanted to speed up the pace. There wasn't a guard in the league quick enough to stay with Webb in the open court. Webb also showed that he could hit the outside jumper when the defender sagged off him. "Forget all that size business," said former NBA guard Calvin Murphy (who was also an All-Star, even though he was only 5-foot-9). "The kid [Webb] is an NBA player."

Webb and Wilkins were major parts of one of the most talented NBA teams in the late 1980s and early '90s. Wilkins eventually became the Hawks' all-time scoring leader, passing Bob Pettit in 1991. But the talented Hawks hadn't won an NBA title, and owner Ted Turner wasn't going to be happy until they did.

WILKENS AT THE HELM

1 9 9 2

Kevin Willis broke club season marks for rebounds (1,258) and rebounding average (15.5).

The early 1990s became a period of transition for the Hawks. As Dominque's stellar career was coming to an end, Atlanta was trying to acquire the right combination of players and coaches to make the team one of the league's elite clubs. Trades were made every year, and players who didn't contribute to the team's chemistry were dealt away for players whom Atlanta hoped would.

The Hawks were impatient for success—they took their best rebuilding step in 1994, when the team hired head coach Lenny Wilkens. Wilkens, a proven winner in the NBA, brought experience to Atlanta, having coached Seattle, Portland, and Cleveland. Wilkens relied on his instincts to tell him which players to keep and which to let go. Atlanta guards Mookie Blaylock and Steve Smith helped push Wilkens to a personal record by the end of the 1995–96 season. Twenty years in the NBA paid off, with Wilkins becoming the first NBA coach to notch 1,000 wins. During that campaign, Wilkens acquired forward Christian Laettner from the Minnesota Timberwolves, and during that off-season, Wilkens added the player who might be the final key to Atlanta's success—All-Star center Dikembe Mutombo.

At 7-foot-2, Mutombo, a native of Zaire, gave Atlanta a powerful force at the center position. "Dikembe anchors the inside defensively, and should make all of our perimeter players better," said general manager Pete Babcock. Coach

Wilkens thought Mutombo could also add to the Hawks offensive output: "He is a guy who can block shots, rebound, and hopefully he'll give us more of an opportunity to run."

Mutombo's full name is Dikembe Mutombo Mpolondo Mukamba Jean Jacque Wamutombo. Mutombo speaks six languages, but he didn't know much about basketball when he was young. "I started to pick up a little bit about basketball in my senior year. I was forced by my older brother who was on the [Zaire] National Team."

Mutombo didn't care much for the game, but gave it another try when he moved to the United States to attend college at Georgetown University, where John Thompson was the head coach. Mutombo credits both Thompson and his early training in soccer for turning him into a big-time basketball player. "Soccer developed my quickness, my feet, and my hands," Mutombo said. "I think another thing that helped me was that I was a goalkeeper. That helped to catch the ball."

Mutombo improved his skills each year he played for Georgetown. During his senior year, he was the Big East Defensive Player of the Year, and set a Big East Tournament record when he grabbed 27 rebounds in a game against Connecticut. He ended his college career as Georgetown's all-time leader in shooting percentage.

The Denver Nuggets had the fourth pick in the first round of the 1991 NBA draft, and they took Mutombo. In Denver, Mutombo earned a reputation as the NBA's best defensive center. He was selected to compete in the All-Star Game twice, and was the NBA's Defensive Player of the Year in 1994–95. He also became the first player in NBA history to

1 9 9 4

Third-year player Stacey Augmon led the Hawks with 333 free throws.

Shot-blocking king, Dikembe Mutombo (pages 26-27).

Steve Smith had the Hawks' best free-throw percentage (.826) for the second season in a row.

lead the league in blocked shots for three years in a row.

Mutombo showed that not only was he a good basketball player, but he was a good person as well. He provided all expenses—including plane tickets—for the Zaire women's basketball team during the 1996 Olympic Games in Atlanta. "Making the money I'm making, it's nice to give something up to help them," Mutombo said. "Some girls came with shoes they had been playing with for two years. In the NBA, I change about 120 pairs a year. I went downtown and got them the shoes the following day. I told them to burn everything they brought with them. I gave them three sets of training stuff, then four pairs of shoes each, and uniforms. They got everything," said Mutombo.

Mutombo's agent called him during the Olympic Games. "You are in the right city," his agent said, "because this is where you are going to play. You are going to be a Hawk." Atlanta had offered Mutombo a five-year contract. But before he would accept it, Mutombo had to call Hawks guard Steve Smith, who was also a free agent. Smith and Mutombo had become good friends when they played against each other in college. "Steve," Mutombo said, "they tell me you must have a big man in Atlanta for you to stay. I am your big man. Don't leave." Mutombo signed his contract, and then Smith signed a new deal with the Hawks a week later.

Mutombo's presence strengthened an Atlanta team that had lost to the Orlando Magic in the previous year's play-offs—mainly because they lacked a strong center who could go up against then-Magic star Shaquille O'Neal. The 1996–97 season showed that Mutombo's dominance in the middle improved the play of his Atlanta teammates. They trusted the

The Hawks' Lenny Wilkens is the NBA's winningest head coach.   29

Mookie Blaylock, Atlanta's offensive and defensive double-threat.

All-Star power forward Christian Laettner.   31

At 7-foot-4, rookie Priest Lauderdale was the tallest player on the Atlanta team.

man behind them, and that trust allowed them to concentrate on their own positions. The guards played better defense, and Christian Laettner was able to play his natural forward position for the first time in his NBA career.

"He [Mutombo] adds to a team that I felt last year had a breakthrough," said coach Wilkens. "We have a real good nucleus."

While Mutombo made the most obvious difference, the Hawks were improved all around, and it was this balance—not the play of any one individual—that made Atlanta virtually unbeatable at home. Not only did the Hawks dominate in the Omni, they also emerged as one of the stongest franchises in the NBA. Many observers around the league felt that the Hawks would provide the best challenge for the powerhouse Chicago Bulls.

The Hawks franchise hasn't won an NBA championship since moving to Atlanta. They've had talented teams, but have never been able to get the job done. If the Hawks' strong showing in the 1996–97 playoffs was any indication of things to come, Hawks fans won't be able to say that for very much longer. With Wilkens at the helm, Mutombo in the middle, and the team's strong play on their home court, the Hawks hope the title of "NBA champ" is one they'll be bragging about soon.